The Adventures of One Man

Jonathan David Valjan

the Peppertree Press
Sarasota, Florida

Copyright © Jonathan David Valjan, 2014

All rights reserved. Published by the Peppertree Press, LLC.
the Peppertree Press and associated logos are trademarks of
the Peppertree Press, LLC.

No part of this publication may be reproduced, stored in a retrieval
system, transmitted in any form or by any means, electronic,
mechanical, photocopying, recording, or otherwise, without prior
written permission of the publisher and author/illustrator.

For information regarding permission,
call 941-922-2662 or contact us at our website:
www.peppertreepublishing.com or write to:
the Peppertree Press, LLC.
Attention: Publisher
1269 First Street, Suite 7
Sarasota, Florida 34236

ISBN: 978-1-61493-290-1

Library of Congress Number: 2014916194

Printed in the U.S.A.

Printed September 2014

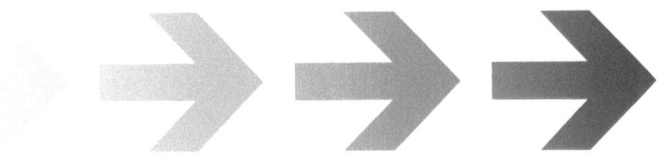

Dedication

I want to thank my parents, whose life experience gave me something to write about. Even though we went through hard times and endured so much, we made it, and this book will tell the world what we had to go through and face just to survive.

May you enjoy it.

Have you ever known someone whose dreams were to turn something repulsive into something exquisite? I have, and I am here to mention the significant story of this dream. Nevertheless, where there are dreams there are also nightmares! Sixteen years I have lived in New York City, Queens to be precise, and it's more like a small city compared to Manhattan. My family and I lived in this apartment building, which was a six-family house, and the street was Fresh Pond Road. It was busy, people were arriving and departing from buses, cars, and trains. At night when you look out your window you can observe your neighbors shouting, screaming, and having parties with music all night.

We lived on the second floor with another vacant apartment next door to us and we knocked it down to enlarge the apartment. When all construction was done, we had five bedrooms, two bathrooms, kitchen, laundry room, living room, dining room, and back yard. My father was in the real estate business, and he saw a property that caught his eye and wanted to invest in it. My father purchased the property and took our family to go see the building, and it was an old factory. As we went inside we saw dust, junk, and garbage everywhere.

My father showed us the basement and mildew seeped through the air and darkness was all around, but the tour wasn't over. He took us to the upstairs apartments and we saw terrible conditions. The floor's carpet was revolting; there were broken windows and lights. Our family worked very hard to clean and remodel the whole building. However, where there are dreams there are also nightmares, and my father's nightmare was having a partner in the building project. His name was Mack Sub. Every day my family and I worked at the property, whether it was shoveling snow or ripping out the cheap carpets.

My father's partner Mack Sub brought doughnuts for us, but he also took matters into his own hands. The project needed some minor things to be taken care of such as cameras, air conditioners, and other necessities.

At the end of the project my father's dream had come true. The property was beautiful, and it shined so bright like the stars in the night sky with the lights turned on at night. When the day came to pay banks and all the other contractors who worked on the project, someone didn't pay up. My father paid the half of money he had but his partner Mack Sub didn't, so the contractors were threatening him, and that's when things changed. Finding out Mack Sub had no cash, the contractors went after my father and threatened to kill him and his family. As all of this was taking place we were in bankruptcy since my father used our apartment as collateral to make his investment and pay some contractors. Living in New York was too expensive. We had to leave as soon as possible. After a great deal of thought we decided to move to Florida. My mother found a home online, and she called up her sister who lives close by to it to check it out for us. We packed our belongings in the moving truck, and my father sold one property in the area and my mother's other sister Lee gave us some money to buy the house in Florida.

    My father and I sat in the truck and my brother, sister, and mother sat in the car. On the road we stopped at hotels and restaurants, and the trip took twenty-four to twenty-eight hours. As we reached Florida we called up my mother's sister, named Maryann, and she let us rest up at her house. The next morning we drove to our new home and the house was on the corner street, and it was amazing the outside was gorgeous.

    As we opened the glass and wood door, we had big smiles on our faces and we walked in the house with tears in our eyes. The house had three bedrooms, two bathrooms, two living rooms, and a laundry room. As we proceeded throughout the house these glass doors came into view, so we opened them and they lead us to a crystal blue pool. With tears and smiles on our faces, we unloaded the moving truck. However, all dreams must come to an end, and sooner or later ours did. My father received a phone call from

Mack Sub and also the contractors. They told him that they would kill him and his family if they didn't receive their money. Some months passed by, and the phone call just sounded like a threat. I was in my last day of high school and I took the bus home.

As I got off the school bus I approached this black limousine on the side of the road. The windows were tinted dark black so I couldn't see inside, so I just walked away. However, I heard a car coming, so I turned my head and this Mercedes pulled beside the limo and two men were talking. As I continued walking, the sky turned gray. It started to rain really hard. As I approached the cross intersection I heard a loud noise sounding like a gunshot. I ran toward the Mercedes, and that's when the man in the limo drove off. I opened the car door and found a man bleeding with his hand on his stomach. The man spoke to me. He said, "My name is Mack Coast. I am an undercover agent for the F.B.I. I was busting a man in the limo for drugs. I have this envelope containing fifty thousand dollars to purchase the drugs from him, but he discovered who I was and shot me." Mack Coast gave me the envelope as he slowly fell asleep in death.

As I was looking at the dashboard in his car I saw a GPS beacon. I pressed it and left the car as I was walking in the pouring rain. I kept thinking to myself if that beacon would reach his department. When I got home I told my parents everything. They called the police and I was questioned for some time. The only thing I didn't tell them was about the money the agent gave me so the police finally left and I got my suitcase ready.

My parents asked me, "What are you doing?" I told them that I had to leave Florida for one year because the man in the limo saw my face and would come looking for me. I showed my parents twelve locations I would be staying at for one month, and the first place was Bermuda. I arrived and checked into a hotel and the next morning I found a fishermen-wanted ad in the local paper. I checked into it and met a man named Bob, and he gave me a job of collecting fish for him to sell to aquariums. Bob was about sixty years old with white hair and a beer belly. He told me I would be starting work today. He gave me a wetsuit and I went to the dock, which was behind his shop. I jumped into the warm water, startling a school of fish as I swam to a small cave. The water was clear from the sun flashing through and the fish were brighter than I ever seen. As I ventured further into the cave it was getting darker, so I had two flashlights on my wetsuit and I turned them on. The light allowed me to get deeper into this cave, and I saw this dark figure approach me. I swam back out of the cave.

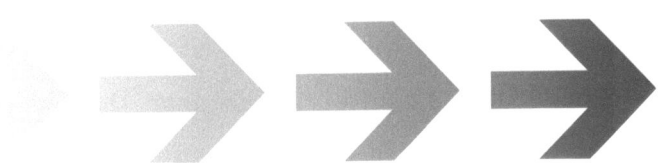

As I came up to the surface I saw two fishermen and I gave them a friendly wave when something stung my leg. I started panicking in the water as the two fishermen grabbed me into their boat. They took me to the beach and placed me on the sand, and that's when I saw this beautiful, lovely, attractive, pretty, appealing, and gorgeous girl standing before me. Her black hair was shining in the golden sun with her skin glowing light brown. She wrapped towels on me to keep me warm and called the ambulance. As I looked at my leg I could see this colorful fish clinging to it, and the pain was getting worse. I was screaming and howling when this girl calmed me down by speaking to me comforting words and telling me that everything will be okay. The ambulance arrived, and I was put on a cot and carried into the vehicle. The emergency room was loud, and I could hear the doctors talking about my situation. I started feeling weak, and my body was trembling; my physical strength was gone. The doctors removed the colorful fish and its spines out of my leg then they began putting pressure on the wound to control the bleeding. The doctors came with a canister of warm water and took my leg and soaked it, but the pain was throbbing. Another doctor brought out this tank and approached my bed. He put a mask on me and I was panicking, my heart beating uncontrollably, and then I just stopped. My eyes were closing and my mind was shutting down, but before I went out the tank next to my bed read "Anesthesia."

    I slept for some time but when I awoke the nurse came in and the doctor right after her. The doctor said, "Good to see you, how are you doing?" I told him I was better, and he said that I had a visitor. This beautiful girl from the beach steps into my hospital room wearing a white blouse with pink shorts. Her lip-gloss was shinning and reflecting the light every time she smiled. She told me her name was Crystal, and she said that she was the lifeguard who saved me. I thanked her as the doctor walked in and said, "Do you want to keep the fish?" I said, "Sure, my boss needs it anyway." And that's when I told Crystal that my name was Jonathan and I was vacationing here and found a fisherman wanted ad in the local paper and that's how I ended up in the hospital. The doctor came in and told Crystal that visiting hours were now over so she got up and started for the exit. I stopped her by saying "wait." She turns around and says, "Is something wrong?" I say, "I was just wondering if you could show me around the island for a while until I can get back on my feet." She smiles and writes her phone number on a piece of paper and says to me "goodnight."

  It was night now, and the hospital was dark and cold, and they had some nurses on shifts but they were too busy to attend to me. I got out of bed, stepping on the cold floor and put on my clothes and grabbed the piece of paper where Crystal wrote her number and left the room. I entered the hallway, and with every step I took I felt the pain in my leg. I reached the administration desk, and there was a man in his late thirties watching the late show and eating chips. He was a physical man, and as I approached him he was startled. I greeted him and he gave me a grin. He gave me a sheet of paper to check myself out and also the bill.

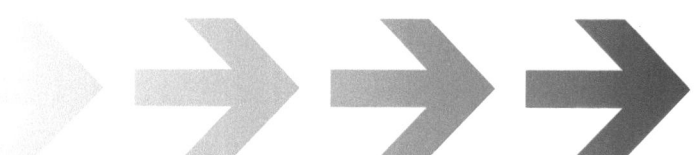

The next day I call Crystal and told her to meet me at the Mexican restaurant on the beach. The food we had was astounding, plus the environment was amazing, right on the beach. I ordered a Fajita with rice and beans. It had a variety of flavors and spices. After that I took her to where I worked and introduced her to my boss, Bob. He said, "What a lovely lady. If a girl like this comes around when you're in the hospital,

The Adventures of One Man

someone check me in." We all laugh and I show Bob the fish that attacked me. He said, "That's a Lionfish; the fins and spines have venom inside to sting their prey." Bob gave me one thousand dollars for the fish, and I told him thanks and that I would be leaving, After all, this was my last week in Bermuda. We all went out to dinner Bob picked the place. It was a seafood restaurant. After all, he was a fisherman and he loved seafood as did we, and after the dinner we left and said our goodbyes to Bob. Crystal and I were walking on the beach, and she started opening up to me, telling me how she originally lived in Puerto Rico but moved here to get away from her father. I asked her why. She said, "Johnny, he started working for this big rich man doing jobs that I don't want to mention. He became greedy, violent. I had to leave; I had no choice." I said, "I am sorry to hear that, but I am happy that I met you and I realized you started calling me Johnny." I told her I didn't mind it, and I walked her to her house. She invited me in and we turned on the TV and sat on the couch. Breaking news covered most of the channels so we turned the volume up and the reporter said, "Florida police found a dead F.B.I. agent in his car. The emergency GPS beacon on the car located the F.B.I. and Florida police are searching for the murderer. The agent was investigating a drug bust when he met his untimely death." Crystal shut the TV off and told me I could sleep on the couch if I stayed, so I agreed and she slept in her room. After all we just met. I didn't think it would be right to sleep with her until I married her, so the sleeping arrangements were fine.

  In the middle of the night I received a phone call on my cell phone from Bob. He said, "Sorry for the late call, but I need you to meet me in the shop. Come alone, okay." I go upstairs and knock on Crystal's door and she opens it and I tell her, "I have to go. Bob just called. I have to see what he wants. He told me to meet him in the shop. I will see you soon, okay." I walk toward the beach up a ramp to Bob's shop. When I reached the front door something was wrong, the lights were off, the place looked deserted. I opened the door and shouted, "Bob, you in here." That's when I heard a faint voice in the back of the shop. I ran and that's when I saw this man throwing a body off the dock into the water. The man saw me and stepped closer, and I remember his face. He was the man in the hospital at the administration desk. I asked him, "Who are you? Where is Bob?" The man tells me, saying, "I am one of the contractors from the project in New York. All the other contractors now work for Mack Sub. He got rich in real estate and in selling drugs and banking. So we all decided to work together to find you and your family and to kill you." He continues, "Bob is dead; that's the body you just saw going off the dock. Now if you don't hand over that drug money, you know the fifty thousand, you will be joining him."

I slowly back away, then run toward the road, but the man tackled me and punched me several times and now I was on the road getting beaten to death. The contractor picked me up and held me by the throat. I was gasping for air and falling in and out of consciousness. However, suddenly he dropped me to the ground. I opened my eyes and in front of me laid the dead contractor on the road. As I looked up I saw Crystal with a scuba tank in her hand. I hugged her and thanked her for saving my life again. The morning approached, and Crystal and I filed a police report about Bob and the dead contractor. The police saw that indeed the fight was self-defense and understood the situation. Crystal drove me to the airport, and I told her after my long trip was over I would come back for her. We kissed and I boarded the plane.

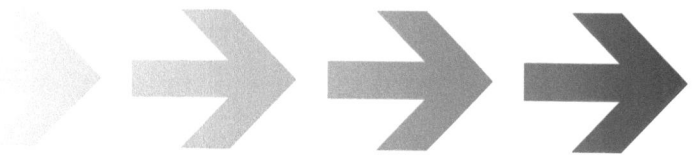

I arrived in the Philippines in the morning and stayed at a cheap motel and applied for a job as a tour guide in a park. A red-headed woman came and gave me the job and told me never to go in the part of the park where it says off-limits. So as a tour guide I showed a few people around, and then when I was done with work I had to check in to the red-haired woman, but I stumbled upon the off-limits sign. I wonder what was in there, so I walked inside and it was magnificent. All kinds of trees, creatures on plants on the ground; however, I was so amazed that I lost track of time and it was dark in the park. Some kind of spider was crawling on my arm. I couldn't scream, I couldn't move, I froze. Then out of the darkness the red-haired woman appeared and shined the flashlight on me and found me and the spider. She took a branch and held it on my arm and the spider went on the branch. As we walk out of the park she screams, "Are you crazy, you could have gotten yourself killed, that's why the sign says off-limits!"

I smile and head back to my motel and I checked my cell phone: thirty missed calls all from my parents. I called them and my dad told me, "Son, the contractors found where we live. They took all your information about your traveling and are going to hunt you down. They tried to kill us but the police came in time and now the police cars are parked outside our house for protection. They are going after you because you are not protected. Please be careful."

I boarded a plane to Puerto Rico and called up Crystal to see if she still had family that I could stay with. She said, "I will call my mom and she will let you stay with her. Okay, see you soon." So that's what happened. Her mom picked me up from the airport and took me to the house and said "mi casa, su casa," or in English my house is your house. Anyway, Crystal's mom talked to Crystal, and her mom was happy I was seeing her daughter and loved that I stayed with her.

The next morning we went to the beach. The water was blue, the sand as white as snow. I asked her why Crystal left this place, and she said, "My family was in poverty. My husband worked for this rich man and got plenty of money. However, he changed; he wasn't the same man I married. He ventured into a room upstairs and never came out. One day I went inside this room and I saw a hit-list of people on white boards, guns, knives; everything that's dangerous was in that room. He caught me in the room and became violent, then the police came and he never came back after that." We went back to the house and she took me to the room, and it was just like she said—nothing changed, everything was still in one place. However, I looked at the white boards and saw something that scared me to death. My picture was on the board! I showed Crystal's mom, and she didn't believe it; I didn't either. How did this get here; that was the question that was mind boggling. The door bell rings and Crystal's mom goes downstairs, and I stay in the room and try to figure out how my picture was on this guy's hit list. After all, we never met.

Lost in my thoughts, I heard a gunshot and I ran downstairs. I saw Crystal's mother lying on the kitchen floor in a pool of blood around her. A voice comes behind me, "She's dead and you will join her."

I turned around only to get smacked in the face and thrown on the kitchen table. I get up and run toward the living room and say, "Who are you?" The man said, "My name is Sunny Lays, I work for Mack Sub, and I am here to take you out." I say, "You must be Crystal's father; why did you kill your wife? She didn't do anything." He says, "Wrong, she was protecting you from me. That's why she took you up to my room, giving you a chance to survive, but you are not armed. How stupid, and now you will die."

    I ran upstairs and locked myself in one of the rooms, and Sunny Lays followed. I hid behind the door as he shot it open, and I tackled him and fought him and then he threw me off him and into the wall. He got up and walked in my direction, and I got up and ran really fast, charging him and me out the second floor window. Glass shattered everywhere as we fell onto the roof, still fighting for survival, and that's when I slipped and fell onto a car. Sunny Lays heads back into the house and I start running down the street and got in a taxi and headed to the airport. I get inside the airport and all I have with me was my wallet and ticket in my pocket. All my clothes were at the house so I had to go back to the house because even my traveling information was there, so I grabbed everything and headed back to the airport.

    I head into the bathroom to clean myself up, and that's when I get the shock of my life. Sunny

Lays walks in and grabs me from behind and throws me into the mirror; breaking glass hits my face. He takes out his gun and starts shooting, breaking lights, and that's when I hid in the stalls. He kicks in stall after stall looking for me. I crawl under the stall and head for the exit until he saw me, and that's when I ran for my life. My flight was to Russia, and I made it on the plane. The flight was long, so I went to the bathroom of the airplane to wash the cuts and blood off my face.

When we landed, I called Crystal and told her about her mom and how her father killed her mom and tried to do the same with me. I told her to stay where she was and I would come for her when I was done with this trip. I went to a restaurant and order smoked fish to go and got an interview as a guard in a museum. The museum had three floors. The first had statues of important origin, the second had weapons of lost cities, and the third was paintings. Every forty five minutes I would check all floors and surveillance cameras for safety precaution. One night I checked the cameras and saw a dark figure on the second floor so I checked it out. I approached the floor and saw glass shattered on the floor. The information box labeled the item as a Chinese sword; it was not in its case. The second floor was quiet, but I heard some noise coming from the third floor so I went up the stairs. As I got into the doorway, I got hit on the head and passed out. I opened my eyes to see Sunny Lays holding the Chinese sword in his hand. He said, "How long will you continue to run from me?" he asked in an aggravated tone. That's when I notice I am tied to a chair. He comes close and asks me, "Where is the envelope? Where is the fifty thousand?" I told him that it was in my suitcase in the hotel I was staying in on the first floor. He swings the sword and slices my cheek. Small drops of blood pour down my face. He says. "I will go to your hotel room on the first floor and if the envelope isn't there I will do a lot more than just cut your cheek." He stabs the sword in the ground and leaves the museum. I try moving close to the sword with the chair and cut the rope off my hands. Now that I am free I call the police to tell them what happened and head to my hotel room. I open my room and clothes were thrown everywhere. My suitcase was ripped open. I went to collect all my belongings and checked out of the hotel. If Sunny Lays noticed I escaped he would still be looking for me. The envelope was in the garbage but the money was in my wallet, so I sent Sunny Lays on a goose chase. However, if he found that out that would mean we would meet again but for now I just went to the airport.

I made my China flight and took a taxi to Beijing to a restaurant to get a job interview. The people there were so nice. Each one there taught me a workout, and I practiced after work and trained hard every day I was off from work. My last week in China came and I was eating dinner in the restaurant when two men walked in. They were wearing black sunglasses and black leather coats. I just kept watching from my seat until they approached me, and that's when things got out of hand. They both approached me and I asked them what they wanted. They opened their cell phone and showed me a picture. The picture was of me and they said that they were hired to find me and turn me over to their boss. One of the men threw me onto a table, then he picked me up and threw me into the glass doors of the restaurant. I fell outside with blood and glass all over me. My friends in the restaurant came and tied up the two men and called the police. However, as I was getting up off the floor Sunny Lays approached me and threw me back into the restaurant. My friends all jumped him and held him down till the police came. The police put the two men and Sunny Lays in a holding cell but late in the night they somehow escaped and disappeared. Anyway, back in the restaurant, we were cleaning all the mess and I apologized for what happened. My friends told me not to worry and gave me food and took me to the airport. They wrote down an address to a place I could stay in my next location, and I thanked them for that.

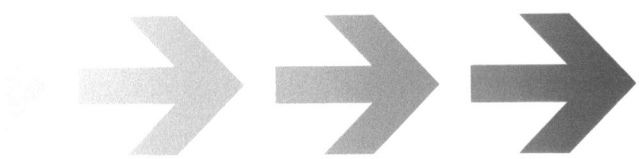

I landed in Japan and took a taxi to the address my friends gave me, and it was an abandoned museum. I stayed there for awhile and slept on the floor with blankets and just toured around Japan for awhile to kill some time just in case Sunny Lays found me. I didn't really have a detailed month in Japan because I was hiding the whole time I was there. I was mostly inside the museum keeping quiet so he wouldn't find me. My next trip I went to was in Vancouver. It was a cold and chilly day. I went to a store to buy clothes and a backpack since my suitcase was slowing me down. I jogged down a dark alley when two raccoons jumped me and stole my wallet. I ran after them. I came to a man in a raincoat and he said, "Like my pets, I trained them to steal." I said, "I want my wallet back, please" and he gave it to me. He said his name was Jack and he was a homeless man. He took me to an abandoned subway station. He said this was his home and if I wanted I could stay here with him. I told him thanks and that if he didn't steal from me

I would provide him with food, so he agreed. After awhile we became good friends, then late at night I received a call from my parents. They said that the F.B.I. were looking for me and Sunny Lays I told everyone that I missed them an I would come back soon.

    As I came back to the subway I saw Jack sitting next to the wall with a bottle of rum in his hand. I approached him and checked his pulse, but nothing. He was dead, but how? As I was gathering my thoughts a voice came behind me and said, "You made it far; too bad everyone you are with ends up dead." As he steps out of the shadows I could see his face; it was indeed Sunny Lays. I ran as fast as I could out of the subway and into a taxi and hurried to the airport.

I was in Colombia, South America, and I worked as a tour guide showing tourists the beautiful waterfalls. Unfortunately, I had to cut my month short because Sunny Lays found me and killed everyone I came in contact with, even the tourists. I took a plane to Canada and took a taxi to Niagara Falls. I could feel the powerful wind and rush of water flying and the tourists snapping photos. I smelled the sizzling hot dogs in the breeze and got myself one. I stayed in a small cottage during the night and shopped during the day. I did this because at night all kinds of animals were walking about. One time I went fishing by the cottage and a black bear chased me and broke down the cottage doors and windows. Anyway, I went back to town and called my parents and told them about what happened. They were happy I was still alive and well. I also told them about Crystal. They were happy for me that I found someone I loved and cared about.

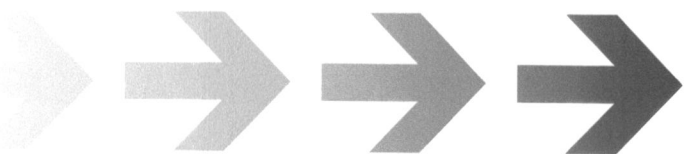

When the month was over I drove to the airport and went to Australia. I met the locals, and they directed me to a petting zoo. I met this woman named Ann, and she showed me this small cottage by a lake and said I could stay there. The next day I went back into town and met a man named Gator. He had snake skin boots and a hat on. He was about fifty years old but had a muscular body, and he told me he hunted crocodiles. He took me on his boat by the cottage on the lake and he said, "Watch closely and keep all hands and feet inside the boat" as he pulled meat out of the cooler and held it towards the water. In a blink of an eye a crocodile jumped out of the water and took it. One was under the boat. Gator looked me in the eye and said, "Swim to shore now!" I look at him and say, "I am not swimming in that water." He was about to push me when the boat tips over and both of us hit the water. With the boat upside down our only way to survive was to swim to shore, but that was about ten feet away and both of us knew we might not make it. Gator said, "Swim; I will stall them." So I swam as fast as I could, and I made it on shore. However, I turned back to see Gator, and he was eaten alive. I ran back to town and told Ann, and we filed a police report and I drove to the airport. As I was parking the rental car I was thinking I could have died if Gator didn't give his life, even though I hardly knew him. He was a good man to give a life for some stranger.

I was in Jamaica and I went in one store to buy some Bob Marley CDs, and I applied for a job teaching tourists how to scuba dive in the reefs. It was difficult to get in the water. The nurse sharks were everywhere around the reefs. The locals told me that they don't really bother humans, maybe rarely. Anyway, it was still scary to be in the water with them. After work I ate in a restaurant off the beach. I had some sizzling spicy shrimp and chicken. I left my table and paid my bill and went for the exit when Sunny Lays came in and he grabbed me. I was in shock. I thought I lost him in my travels, but he grabbed me and threw me into a table and I fell, knocking food and silverware and dishes all over the floor. The restaurant owner called the police but Sunny Lays didn't care. He kicked me in the stomach, making me vomit the food I just ate. He walked me to the second floor window of the restaurant and dropped me. I fell into the restaurant pool. I swam out of the pool and limped into a taxi and took a plane to the Caribbean. I was still teaching tourists how to scuba dive, and I went to the location where I had a class to start. I put on my scuba gear as I heard footsteps approaching. As I turned I got smacked in the face and fell into the water. Now in the water I turned my head to see who smacked me and it was Sunny Lays. No matter where I go, he somehow finds me. He jumped in the water and swam after me. I swam to the reefs and sharks were there, so I just stood there hoping he wouldn't follow me.

As I looked at Sunny Lays I could see the fear in his eyes and he tried to swim for shore, but the sharks

The Adventures of One Man

sensed something so they charged at him and ripped his leg clean off. Blood was everywhere in the water. I looked closely at these sharks and realized that these were bull sharks. I panicked and swam for my life but one of the sharks charged at me too and grabbed my leg. I could hear the bones in my leg crack like a toothpick. I took the scuba tank off me and started pounding the shark with it and it finally let me go. I swam to the shallow water, and one of the lifeguards saw me and rushed toward me. However, the shark came back and grabbed my leg again and was pulling me into deep water. The lifeguard came, smacking the shark. The shark let me go, but now I couldn't feel the pain in my leg. I couldn't feel anything. The lifeguard called for an ambulance, and I was in the emergency room. Doctors removed whatever was left of my leg so I wouldn't get an infection. Two weeks later I received my prosthetic leg for my left leg, and after several therapy classes I took a plane to Bermuda.

I called up Crystal and we got together and walked on the beach, and the sun was setting and the clouds were orange and pink. Dolphins were jumping out of the ocean into the horizon I looked into Crystal's eyes and bent my right leg and asked, "Will you marry me?" with the ring box open, shining in the dim light. She said yes, and I told her how I bought a house in Puerto Rico and we could live there since she liked it so much. Crystal became a lifeguard on the beaches there and I became a firefighter. As I fell asleep the doorbell rang and I awoke and Crystal brought this package that was on our door step. There was a letter on it, and Crystal read it, and this is what it said: *"Dear Jonathan, long time no see. I just wanted to wish you a happy marriage. I hope you like the gift I have to offer you. After all, I am your father-in-law."* I opened the package to find two small dead sharks and a piece of someone's foot. Crystal was screaming and crying. I held her tight, comforting her. It was late at night; I couldn't sleep. I was up all night thinking, how could Sunny Lays survive; he was eaten alive, or was he?

The next day Crystal and I filed a police report about Sunny Lays, and they hooked us up to the F.B.I. After all, they were still looking for us. The F.B.I. gave me a private line to connect to them and private number as well, which I stored in my

The Adventures of One Man

cell phone. The next day I came home from work and walked into the kitchen and found Crystal tied up to a chair with a gun pointed at her head. Sunny Lays said, "I have a reputation to keep, and the man I work for wants you dead, Jonathan, and those who get in the way will die." I yelled, "She is your daughter; what's wrong with you!"

Then I ran to the living room and called the F.B.I. number on my cell phone and told them, "Come now, Sunny Lays will kill me! I live at 71-20 Beach Street!" They said they were coming, so I ran outside and shut the power off in the house. I took my hand axe out of the car and ran back into the house and stepped into the kitchen. Sunny Lays was close. I heard him say, "Shutting off the power might give you a chance of survival," and then I saw him go outside. I ran to Crystal and cut the ropes off her and told her to take the car and get the police, so she went outside. The power in the house came back on, and that's when I realized why Sunny Lays was not in the house. He had turned on the generator. I ran outside. I saw him hold Crystal by the throat, about to strike her with a knife. I ran and tackled him, jabbing the axe in his leg. After all, he only had one leg; the other the shark ate.

Crystal went inside the car, but Sunny Lays took out his gun and blew out the windshield, making glass shatter all over Crystal and the car. I punched him and yelled for Crystal to drive and get help fast, so she did. She left the driveway and I ran back inside the house. I ran to the back of the house because the beach was our backyard, and I dove into the water to hide. I saw Sunny Lays follow, and limping onto the beach. The axe still stuck in his leg, he is searching for me and then all of a sudden I hear police sirens. He doesn't know what to do so he jumps into the water. I swam toward shore but he saw me and grabbed me. The police were in our house, and some came onto the beach, flashing lights in our direction, and saw what was happening. Some shot at us, and the bullets hit Sunny Lays and he fell back into the water. I swam toward shore. The police were going to arrest Sunny Lays, but with the blood in the water due to his leg the sharks dragged him to his death. Crystal and I never forget that night, but now we were happy that it was finally over.

After I married Crystal we had two daughters, and they were beautiful. Crystal was attending to them as I received a phone call and the voice that came on was Mack Sub. I was in shock but I said, "How did you get this number?" He said, "My assassins and contractors are not the only ones trained to kill and find people. I am also. I will come to Puerto Rico and take everything you have, starting with your family." I hung up the phone and told Crystal everything, and we both decided to move to Florida.

    I called the F.B.I. and told them everything about the call and why we had to move, so they put us on the witness protection program and moved us to Old Englewood Village in Florida. We had a house with two floors. Everything was paid for, and the F.B.I. told us they will put cameras everywhere except the bathrooms. So that's how they would watch us if anything happened. Anyway, I called up my parents, and they visited us in our house and they met Crystal and our baby daughters. I told them how sorry I was for not calling them sooner and told them about our situation and how I got a fake left leg and other stories from my trip. I told them how the F.B.I. are helping protect us from Mack Sub and how we have been through so much just to survive. They were happy that I had grown up and took care of my family. They said that Mack Sub called them and told them that he is no longer after them, only their first-born son. Since I was their first-born son, I was scared out of my mind. After all, if Sunny Lays was so tough to beat, how hard would Mack Sub be?

My parents said that the police and F.B.I. will find him and stop him, so I was at ease just a little. Anyway, at least my parents, brother, and sister were safe from this monster. I told my parents thanks for visiting us and told them how much I loved them. As the night pressed on, I received 15 phone calls and finally a voice came on which said, "Hi Jonathan, remember me? This is Amanda. We went to junior high together; don't you remember, sexy?" The next morning I told Crystal about the phone calls and how that girl who knew me was just creepy. Crystal took my daughters to my mom's house as I stayed home to relax. She said she would be home soon; after all, it was only a 15-minute trip from here to their house. I am upstairs on my bed when I received a phone call. I answer and a voice comes on and says, "Sexy, sorry to wake you, I am here, please let me in." I ask, "Who is this?" That's when the voice said, "Amanda." I get up off the bed and look out the window, and I see her smiling at me. I call the F.B.I., and they said they would send agents over in 10 minutes, so I ran downstairs to see if the door was locked and it was. I looked out the window but she wasn't there, and that's when I heard her voice. I turned my head to see her on the couch say, "Room for two, baby." I was in shock. I asked her, "How did you get in; the door was locked?" She said, "Don't be shy. It was open, and then when I came in I locked it" I walked toward the kitchen, and she got up and followed.

    She said, "You know, Jonathan, in junior high school I loved you, but you didn't notice me so I stalked you, and now since we're together I will kill you!" I don't move, I am just in shock of what was happening, and that's when she takes out this 7-inch knife and stabs my right leg. I fall to the floor in pain and look up at her. She's smiling at me. Blood is pouring out, and that's when I hear my front door get kicked down. F.B.I. agents flooded the house, and Amanda turned herself in. The first aid agents came and patched my wounds up. They said they were glad that I called them, because the cameras weren't working due to the weather they had. A few minutes later Crystal walks in and the agents tell her what had happened, and she comes to me and says she was sorry for not being here to help me. I told her I was fine, the agents saved me. And that's when one of the agents said, "This girl was in the mental institution until she somehow escaped, so it's a good thing we found her before she did something even worse." I thank the agents and tell them to check the cameras again before they leave. It was getting late now and Crystal wanted to pick up our daughters by my parents house, so she took her car and I took my 2009 red Dodge Charger and followed her there.

  I wanted to drive my car and she wanted to drive her car, so that's why we didn't go together. However, during the 10 minutes of driving this black car was coming head on in Crystal's direction, so I called her and told her to take the back road to my parents' house and she did. The black car was still coming, and as she turned, the car smacked into my front bumper and instant car crash. The windshield exploded, my seatbelt broke, and blood and glass were all over me. The engine was on fire on the hood of the car as I opened the door and fell on the road. Crystal saw the accident and came back with her car to see what happened to me, and other cars stopped and called the police to report the accident. The guy in the black car came out and had a gun to my head, and this is what he said, "A limo is coming. You will come with me and we will see Mack Sub." I was on the floor, but witnesses saw what was happening, and even my wife saw. She was screaming and running in my direction, but it was too late. The limo came, I was thrown inside, and we took off. We headed to this abandoned gas station on Dearborn Street 5 minutes from where I live. I was walked inside the small building and chained to the wall. My t-shirt was ripped, showing off my six-pack abs; however, I was at their mercy because the crash was still affecting me.

Then Mack Sub comes out of the dark station and says, "The first born of your parents—you know you are one hard person to kill. I mean I send in assassins, crazy girls like Amanda, and even your father-in law, and you still won't die. That's why I decide to go after you first. With you gone that will make your parents mourn, and then they will pay for what happened to me in the New York project." I with some breath in me say, "Let it go, Mack, its history. You don't have to do this. You don't have to kill." He smiled and said, "It's too late for me to change. Once I take you out, my life will be complete, and only then your parents will feel what I felt and understand what they did to me." I answer him back saying, "You did everything. My parents did nothing. You made yourself this way; blame yourself, not my parents." Mack Sub didn't like that remark. He punched me several times in my abs and then in my face. I was out cold but I still heard what was happening, and that's when I heard sirens. I opened my eyes and the F.B.I. was in the gas station aiming guns at Mack Sub and his men. They handcuffed all of them, got me into an ambulance, and that's where they told me something.

The Adventures of One Man

What they told me was that the police were checking out the crash. One of them said, "Crystal told them what happened to you and she saw the limo go back to Englewood, so when we arrived at the scene we drove and saw the black limo in the gas station, and that's how we found you. By the way, the governor wrote a check of one million dollars for your bravery and helping us get Mack Sub. The money will be put directly into your bank account, and also you have been offered to become an F.B.I. agent and you are having dinner with the governor tonight." I thanked the agent as they drove me back to my house. I told Crystal everything, and she and my daughters came with me to the governor's house. The governor was very proud and happy that Mack Sub was out of our lives, and the dinner he had for us was great. As the dinner was over the governor got a call from the F.B.I. and they told him to turn on the news.

So he did, and breaking news was all over TV. The reporter said, "Mack Sub was being transferred to a secure prison in an armored truck and escorted with 3 police cars. However, according to the footage we received from the F.B.I., there was an ambush and

Mack Sub escaped. All police personnel escorting him were dead at the scene." The governor shut off the news and looked at me. He said, "You are an F.B.I. agent. If you are in trouble, call this number, and I will call the agents to protect you. They will come in 5 minutes or less." The governor tells me to meet him at an agency meeting tomorrow. It's for all agents, and he will talk about what happened on the news.

    The governor said, "Someone in this agency is leaking out information to the press and to Mack Sub's men. That's how the ambush happened. What I want to know is who and why?" The agents all leave as do I, and that's when I receive a call on my cell phone. The governor is in the room with me and is watching me as I put the phone on speaker mode. The voice said, "Jonathan, Mack Sub here. I just can't kill you. I mean I get so close and then the F.B.I. takes you away. By the way, I know the governor is listening, so let me tell him that there is a traitor in the F.B.I., and that's how I got your number. You see, with money and persuasion anybody can turn from good to bad. One day I will come out of hiding and take you out, Jonathan, but like I said, one day." and the phone line goes dead. The governor and I look at each other and I say to him, "We will bring this monster to justice, and if he wants me dead, then he will have to come out of hiding." I tell the governor good night as I head home and tell Crystal everything about work. She was scared. I was too, but I told her one day Mack Sub will be captured and will pay for the crimes he has committed. However, one day I will have to face him again, but like I said, one day.

To be continued.

It has been ten years since Mack Sub's phone call, and no one has seen him. I am thirty years old, and I retired from the fire department and F.B.I. agency because of my prosthetic left leg. Even though I spent weeks at rehab ten years ago and trained myself, the two jobs were taking so much out of me. The traitor inside the F.B.I. was found to be the leader of the agency. He went on a cruise to disappear from authorities. My wife Crystal and two daughters went on the same cruise ship, and once the leader and traitor found them he blew up the whole ship.

The ship sank to the ocean floor, and news reports and search parties found no survivors. As I found out, I was in agony. My friends and family comforted me, but I couldn't cope with the loss of my dead family. Many of my friends and family showed up to the funeral and gave their condolences.

The F.B.I. found that there was a traitor, and he was working with Mack Sub. After that the agency was under investigation. Outside the funeral home a man approached me, and his name was Michael Bay.

He said, "I have an assignment for you. I represent a wealthy and powerful man, and he wants you to collect some live creatures for him." He gave me a list of creatures his representative wanted me to catch. The first on the list was a Great White shark, King Cobra, Crocodile, Hippopotamus, and the white Rhinoceros. He said, "On this trip will be 40 skilled men hunters, and gear and technology will be provided to catch these creatures." I told him I wasn't interested. He looks at me and says, "The man I represent will make you, one way or another force you to do this." Michael Bay gets into a black limo and leaves as I go home to think about what he said to me.

I go on my laptop and research the web for the Great White shark, and I was amazed how it could smell blood in the water three miles away. I learned that speed was its best weapon as it attacks first and then circles to finish off its prey. It can grow to 20 feet and weigh 7 thousand pounds and is found in the Mediterranean, Africa, and Australia. It rolls back its eyes for protection before it attacks, and as it grabs its prey it thrashes its head side to side, sawing the prey with its teeth.

The next creature I looked at was the King Cobra. It can grow 16 feet; it lives in China and Southeast Asia, where bamboo provides shelter, its nest, and hunting grounds. It can be found in abandoned buildings in villages, and the common name for it is snake-eater. It strikes rapidly with fangs injecting venom that paralyze the nervous system of prey. It's active by day, collecting scents in the air with its tongue.

I looked at the Crocodile next, and it can grow 20 feet, weighing 2 thousand pounds. It can hide underwater for more than an hour and lives in Africa: the Nile River and Madagascar. It has a muscular tail which is used as a weapon for knocking prey to the ground. It rips off the prey and stores the remains underwater. In the Bible it is called Leviathan, king of the beasts. The next creature was the Hippopotamus and it lives in Africa in rivers, lakes, swamps, and the power in its jaws can pierce the armor of a Crocodile in one bite. It can grow to 15 feet and weigh 8 thousand pounds, feeding on plants and grass. It is also said to charge at boats or canoes if it feels like its baby is threatened.

    The last creature I studied was the white Rhinoceros, which also lives in Africa, and I was amazed how it was said to attack trucks. It has rough skin and a large center horn that can grow to 5 feet. The horn is made out of compressed hair, but what amazed me was that this animal can eat peacefully but without warning attack. The next day I went to buy a red Dodge Charger since I had no car. I went to a Chinese buffet, and the waitress was very attractive. I was amazed how beautiful this Chinese woman was. She had long black hair and a white smile as she asked me what I wanted to drink. I drank lemonade and ate black pepper chicken, 3 plates; it was the best. I paid my bill and left her a 20 dollar tip and thanked her for serving me and told her I would be back soon. I drove my car to the beach and parked it as I walked on the sand.

    I was thinking about the Chinese woman; I couldn't get her out of my head. Then I was thinking of my dead family, Crystal and my two daughters. How could I think about another woman when I just lost my family? Even though my family died I didn't want to be alone. I needed someone to talk to, someone to love. My family and friends supported my decision and said it was not good for me to be alone. I went to the Chinese buffet, and the same waitress was there and she sat me where I usually sat and I ate.

It was a slow day. I was the only customer eating. The waitress came over and took my plate and poured me some more lemonade. I asked her if she would sit and join me. She told her boss and then he approached my table. He was an old Chinese man. He sat down and said, "You like this place, you come every day, you are a good customer. I see you also like the waitress here too." I say, "Yes I do. May she dine with me?" The old man said, "This is my daughter." I say, "She is beautiful; may I please dine with her?" The old man said, "This is the first time I see a gentleman." I told him thank you, and he leaves the table and brings his daughter.

I tell her my name and how happy I am to meet her father. Then she asked me, "Why do I always see you here alone and sad?" I told her what happened to my family, and she said she was sorry. I told her how I enjoy Chinese food and also talking to her. She smiles, and we talk about life and how I got my prosthetic leg. I also told her how I was a firefighter and F.B.I. agent until I retired. After I stopped talking she said her name was Meizhen, which means beautiful pearl.

Her father came and said, "You are very nice man, but the store is closing. You must go." As I was leaving the table Meizhen gave me her phone number. I went inside my car and called up my parents and friends and told them about the Chinese woman. They were all happy for me. Meizhen and I dated for a year and then got married on the beach. I was so happy that I found someone I loved. We moved into a condominium on Englewood Beach in Florida.

I drove to the buffet one day, but something was wrong. Police lights were flashing. I got out of the car and officers approached me. They said, "A man named Michael Bay was here and shot and killed everyone inside the buffet. He was seen leaving with a Chinese woman." I told the police that this man threatened me before. The officers assured me that

The Adventures of One Man

they will find him and get my wife back. The killing was all over the news, and my parents and friends drove to the funeral home to comfort me there. As I approached my car a man came from behind; he was Michael Bay. I punched him and threw him to the ground, but then a black limo drove by and the door opened.

Michael Bay said, "This is the man I represent." The man walked out of the limo, and it was Mack Sub. I just froze. It was like a nightmare never ending. Mack Sub came closer to me and said, "I have been thinking 10 years how to make your life fall apart, and then it hit me. I had a guy on the inside of the F.B.I., and he gave me all your information about where you work, eat, what you study. This man was on the cruise ship not to disappear from the cops but to do one more job for me. Your wife Crystal and two daughters were on the ship, he found them, and he blew up the ship. He killed himself in the process, but finished his job. I like a man who can put his work ahead of anything." I was about to smash Mack Sub into the ground when Michael Bay tied up my hands with rope and forced me in the limo.

Inside the limo Mack Sub is talking and he said, "My assistant told you about the creatures I want to collect, and he also told you that if you didn't cooperate you would be forced to do the job one way or another. I was amazed how you were able to get remarried and start a new life. Too bad you put more people's lives endanger. It's a shame her whole family had to die because of you. Your wife is alive for now. She will only stay that way if you do what I ask." The limo stops and Michael Bay cuts the rope off my hands and gives me the list of creatures. Mack Sub said, "Jonathan, there will be 40 hunters with you on this trip. Jeeps, planes, and ships are provided to get what I want. You will be leaving in two days." Michael Bay closed the limo door as they drove off, leaving me by my car. I drove to the police station and told them what happened. They said to go along with the plan until they figured out how to track him. Then I told my family and friends, and they couldn't believe Mack Sub was still alive. After all, he was at least in his 60s. We all thought he was dead. The two days came fast, and Michael Bay came and gave me a contact number to reach him when the job was done. He took me in the limo to Mack Sub's hideout, and the 40 men were there with gear, technology standing by Mack Sub's side. He introduced me to everyone and showed us the cargo planes we would be taking. There were two cargo planes and we got on them and headed to China for our first creature, the King Cobra.

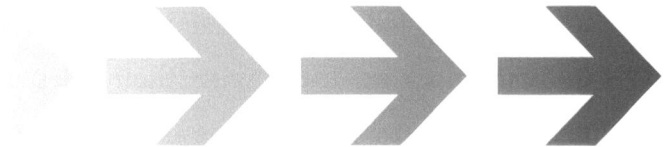

As the plane landed, we drove jeeps to an abandoned village where the locals saw sightings of the Cobra. Five hunters went inside a small village house and turned on their night vision glasses with flashlights. They saw the Cobra but reacted too slowly, and the snake strikes and injects venom in two hunters. The third hunter grabbed the snake and put it into a suitcase. We left the two hunters there because they died from the snake bite. After all, there was no hospital. I felt terrible leaving them there, but the hunters wanted to catch these creatures and receive their money from Mack Sub.

    The cargo plane was now headed for Africa, which made all our lives easy since almost all the creatures were in Africa. As we set the plane down we all decided to get a cage ready for the Crocodile. We put meat in the cage, and eventually one came close to the cage and he got stuck inside. Ten hunters came and attached the cage to the jeep but once that happened the Crocodile was calling for help. Two Crocodiles go on land and chase the five hunters, smacking them with their tales. All the hunters fall to the ground. They all get dragged into the water and ripped apart and eaten alive.

    The Crocodile in the cage was getting aggressive, so the hunter dropped in a small capsule and the creature instantly fell asleep. He explained to me that once the capsule is broken, sleeping gas seeps out and puts anything to sleep, and he gave me some. The next day we went back to the same river, and five hunters and I drove the jeeps to the location of the Hippopotamus. They go in the water and shoot at the beast, but it goes under the water. So I head back and get a small boat for the hunters.

Five hunters are on the boat, and I am in the jeep watching with binoculars them trapping a baby Hippopotamus. The mother comes out of the water and bites down on the small boat, leaving the five hunters in the water. They try to swim, but the current is strong and it's too late. The Hippopotamus killed them all in its jaws. I drove back to the cargo plane and told the rest of the hunters what happened, and we took off to our next location—getting the white Rhinoceros.

There was tall grass in the savanna, but we found what we were looking for and we chased it with our jeeps. The hunters closed and trapped the Rhino, making a triangle with the jeeps. The Rhino charged and smacked the jeep upside down, trapping five hunters. It kept charging until the jeep blew up and killed the hunters inside. The assault didn't stop. It charged at the second jeep, exploding the engine, and that killed another five hunters. The third jeep I was in had five hunters inside, but they left the jeep and went on foot to attack the rhino. The 5-foot horn on the rhino smashed the hunters to the ground. All the hunters died. I took the jeep back and told the 13 hunters the story about what happened. They took the cargo planes to the sky.

 I was on the first plane with five hunters. The second plane had 8 hunters, a King Cobra, and a Crocodile. There was thunder, lighting, and rain. The second cargo plane took a nose dive into the ocean because of the bad weather. Everything on the plane died in the water. The five hunters and I begin talking about how so many died and we came back with nothing. They said, "Why are you here?" I told them how Mack Sub kidnapped my wife and will kill her if I don't get these creatures to him. The five hunters were angry, and even though we had the Great White shark to catch the hunters cancelled the mission. They were so upset with so much death this adventure caused them that they couldn't continue.

 I drove my red Dodge Charger and the five

hunters took the jeep as we met Michael Bay at the funeral home. The black limo pulls in and he steps out. The hunters tell him about the mission and how it was a complete failure to start with. Michael Bay looks at me and says, "I guess you can say goodbye to your wife then," and heads back to the limo, but before he does the five hunters tackle him and open a sleeping capsule. As Michael Bay awakens, I ask him, "Where is my wife?" He doesn't answer, so I say, "These five hunters will kill you for putting them through that death adventure, and I can't stop them." Michael Bay finally snaps and says, "Mack Sub is in an auto dismantling yard," so we drive there.

    The five hunters draw their guns on Mack Sub and he says, "Wow, you made the whole trip; it was to see how many would survive. Anyway, do you know where we are? We are at an auto yard, and the machines here are called car crushers. What you see above your heads is a car magnet," and it gets turned on and lifts the jeep. Then Mack Sub controls the lift and releases the jeep on the five hunters, killing them. Then Mack Sub approaches me and says, "What amazes me is your bravery. You are not scared of me, and I can't seem to kill you."

I asked him, "Where is my wife?" He said, "She is at a dock on Boca Grande, Florida; the dock will explode, sinking her to the bottom of the deep water. She is inside a locked car, tied up with handcuffs on hands and feet." I take out the sleeping capsule and break it and throw it on Mack Sub. He gets knocked out and I carry him in my car. We drove to the beach where he said she would be, and I called the police and an ambulance. Mack Sub awakened and realized that he was confined in handcuffs. I pull the car up, and I see the car on the dock. I ran to her, but the explosion went off. The car drops into the water. I head back to my car and pull out an axe and dive into the deep water. I broke the side of the windows in the car and grabbed my wife and swam to the surface. She was unconscious. I performed chest compression. The ambulance and police came and took Mack Sub to a holding prison. The ambulance took my wife to the emergency room. After 5 minutes I was able to see her. She was doing well. I told her about Mack Sub and how the police have him in custody. The next day the news reports said that Mack Sub was put not in a jail but in a mental institution, being treated for his mental condition.

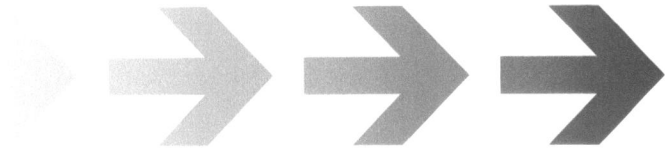

The Chinese buffet was open again, and my wife was in charge of it. My wife and I also had a baby boy. With the months passing by our baby boy grew up fast. His name was Gan, which means adventure. By the time he was 10 years old he had the body of a body builder. We trained him to eat healthy and work out, and that made him strong. After months gone by I received a phone call from the mental institution. It was Mack Sub.

He said, "I will get out of here. After all, money talks; how do you think I got this number and am able to make a call directly to you? Just imagine what I can do once I get out of here. Well, I have to go, but remember, wherever you go, I will find you and I will kill you." After the phone call I told my wife and son everything they needed to know about Mack Sub and my violent past with him. I told them how he was 75 years old and still trying to kill me. My wife made plans to sell everything we have in Florida and move to China. So that's where this adventure continues, in China.

To be continued.

My wife Meizhen and son Gan and I sold everything we owned in Florida. My bank account had two million, dollars due to the one million the governor gave me from before and another million from what we sold. We had enough money to buy a penthouse suite in Hong Kong, China. Several months passed by, and I called my parents to tell them why we had to move without saying goodbye to them. I missed them and my other family members dearly, but if we still lived in the United States I knew that my family would be endangered.

    My son worked for the secret technology unit of China, and he would come home every night very late from work. So Meizhen and I went to a late dinner and a movie. After all that, we drove home and it was eleven o'clock at night. We opened our door and turned on the lights to find a man with a gun in his hand. He was a Chinese man about fifty-five years of age and he spoke English to us. He said, "You two sit on the chairs next to the table." Meizhen and I followed his demands. He then approached me and shot me in my stomach and then he shot me in my shoulder. He said, "If you move or try to fight you will die," as he handcuffed my hands and feet to the chair.

He then turns to Meizhen and says, "Do you remember me?" She shakes her head no, and then he pulls out a chair and sits down next to us. He continues, "When we were teenagers we had an arranged marriage, but your family moved to America to start a new life and you joined them. Now I see you married an American man, and you left me and my parents with shame and embarrassment. I felt all this anger, hate, and betrayal, so I became a Ninja assassin when I was young and moved to America to find you. I couldn't find you but I found a man who helped me, and his name is Mack Sub. He made me what I am today. He helped me find you, and now I must repay him by getting rid of you."

I was in too much pain to reason with him, but Meizhen tried by saying, "Please forgive me; I am sorry for what I have done. Please let us go." The man points the gun at Meizhen and said, "You're forgiven," and shot her twice. The man approaches me and says, "Your wife is dead and you will soon join her," as he takes out a detonator from his pocket. He says, "This entire building is wired with explosive bombs. Mack Sub told me to make sure you're dead, so by making a building fall on you there is no chance you will survive. Unfortunately, since the entire building has to come down other people will die, but that's what happens when you mess around with Mack Sub. By the way, when I am done with you I will hunt down your son Gan and I will kill him."

  The man smiles as he walks out of my penthouse. I try to move, but I am stuck to the chair with the handcuffs. I was losing blood due to the gunshot wounds, and that's when I gave up hope. I gave up the will to survive as the clock hit eleven thirty–five. The explosion went off and the building came down. Gan came home from work and saw the police cars, fire trucks, and ambulances everywhere. Debris was all over the cars and streets so he went up to a police officer and asked him, "What happened?

Where is my home?" The police officer said, "The entire building was blown up. Everyone that was inside is dead." Gan was in shock. He told the officer that his parents were in there, but the police officer said again, "There are no survivors." Gan stayed at a hotel for the night just to cope, sleep, and realize what happened that night.

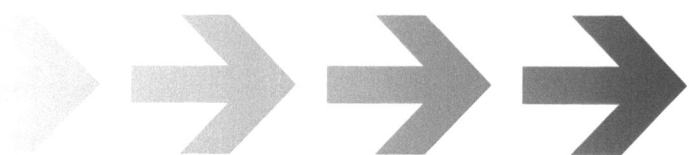

The next day news reporters were talking about the building falling down, killing at least five hundred people. Police reports were out on missing people, and the news was so terrible that Gan just shut it off. Gan went to work, and a lawyer approached him about his parents' will, and the will said to give everything to Gan. The two million dollars in the bank account was transferred to Gan's account. Gan talked to the Chinese government about the secret technology unit. He wanted to buy what they were making. The government told Gan that the product would cost five hundred thousand dollars. Gan told them to paint it the color gold. The Chinese government told Gan that "this product is a suit; it can withstand any man-made weapon. The suit is light weight for easy activity, and inside the helmet has infrared technology which seeks out anyone or anything hiding that is retaining heat. The suit also has built-in taser sensors all over the suit, so whoever touches you when wearing the suit will get an electrical shock making them immobilized for a short time."

Gan told them that he wanted two suits, and the price went up to one million dollars. The two suits were knight suits but had muscles imprinted on them, making it look like body armor. Gan took the two suits and told the Chinese government he would be living in America. The Chinese government told Gan, "Never tell anyone about these suits, and by the way, these suits have no weakness so once you put it on nothing can kill you." The Chinese government asked Gan, "Why do you need these suits; you are not a soldier?" Gan told them, "Someone murdered my parents. They blew up an entire building just to kill them, and I want to bring the murderer to justice."

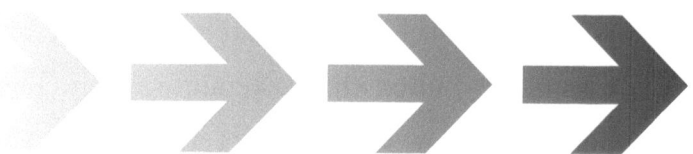

Gan took a plane to the United States and went to Florida. He told his grandparents and other relatives what happened to his parents in China. He told them how he decided to move to Central America, Guatemala City. Everyone wanted Gan to stay in Florida, but he wanted to live far away from any family so they wouldn't be targeted. Gan moved to Zone 10 in Guatemala City, called Zona Viva. Its district had bars, restaurants, hotels, shopping malls, and office buildings. Gan lived in a hotel since he had the money to do so.

Gan watched the news reports about the city and a reporter said, "Police are inexperienced and underpaid, and crime has increased in the city." As the reporter was announcing the information, the

The Adventures of One Man

news channel was disconnected. Gan walked out of his hotel room and went to the lobby of the hotel, but as he was heading out the doors a man came and stopped him. Gan turned and noticed how this was the man from the news channel. The man said, "You must be new here. Let me tell you something about this place; the government is corrupt they get paid off every day from drug lords. Drug smugglers and mobsters compound to high crime rates. Tourists are robbed, raped, and even murdered." Gan asked the man, "What happened to the news channel; why was it suddenly disconnected?" The man said, "The government is corrupt. If anyone broadcast the truth about something they are fired or killed."

Gan is about to speak to the man when a bullet hits the man in the forehead. Screams carry on in the hotel, and Gan looks for the shooter but doesn't find one. Gan goes back to his hotel room and thinks about what the now-dead news reporter told him. Gan decides that this was the time to put on the suit and clean up the city. The two suits were in a suitcase under the bed, and as he was about to reach for it he receives a phone call from the hotel phone. A man's voice came on and told him, "Your parents are dead and you're next. Meet me in the hotel lobby and we will talk." Gan hangs up the phone and heads to the lobby. Gan is inside an elevator when a man comes in and this man turns to Gan and says, "So you're the child of Meizhen." At that moment Gan knew this was the man who killed his parents. Gan throws the first punch, and the man smiles and blocks it saying, "I am amazed how you were able to know what I did from just the mention your mother's name."

Gan and the man fight as the elevator slowly goes down to the lobby. The elevator doors open, and the man threw Gan out into the lobby. The man came out and picked up Gan and threw him at the hotel's front desk. Gan gets up and just stands, not moving but waiting for the man to make the first move. Gan yells to the man, "Who hired you to kill my parents?" The hotel staff is calling the police, and a group of people in the hotel are watching Gan and the man fight. The man charges at Gan, but misses and smacks into glass doors. Gan approaches the man and picks him up by the shirt and yells,

"Who hired you to kill my parents?" The man finally shouts "Mack Sub" and passes out on the floor. Gan couldn't believe what he heard. How was it even possible for Mack Sub to locate him?

The police came and Gan told them everything about the fight and the murder of his parents, and the police took the man to jail. Gan finally brought this man to justice. After all the commotion Gan went back to his hotel room and called back the Chinese government on his private cell phone. He said "I need a Dodge Viper sports car, copper red, and I need small taser sensors all over it, and it can only open when I say a password." The Chinese government worked on the sports car and shipped it by plane to Gan's location. Gan drove the car inside the hotel's parking lot, and if anyone would try to steal it or touch it without saying the password they would get a small charge of electricity.

Gan wired the house with sensors, and if anyone touched the house without a password the house would go into lock-down mode. Lock-down mode closed and protected the house in a steel shutter cage. Gan installed a secret room in his garage, where he put two of his knight suits. Gan turned on the news, and the reporters said, "Tourists, beware of the danger at night." Gan shut off the TV and realized that many people never went out at night due to the high crime. Gan wanted to change that, and he also wanted to put all of Mack Sub's men behind bars. It was eleven o'clock at night, and Gan decided that this was the night he would clean up the city. Gan went into his secret room in the garage and put on the knight suit and went inside his Dodge Viper sports car.

    He drove into the city and turned on his infrared or heat seeker technology and saw the drug smugglers in progress. He videotaped what was going on, and he left the recording on the dashboard as he got out of the car. Street lights were off outside, and the drug smugglers saw a dark figure approaching them. The six men took their guns and were shooting at Gan, but then they all stopped. The men didn't believe what they saw: no blood, no bullet holes, not even a dent. They started moving back slowly, but Gan charged at them. As soon as his suit touched them the tasers sensors went off, shocking the men. Five men were immobilized on the ground from the jolts of the taser; the sixth was shaking with his gun pointed at Gan. He asked, "Who are you?" Gan approached the man and said, "I am the Golden Knight and I am cleaning up this city." The man from fear passed out.

 He then takes all the drugs and lights a match, burning everything till there is no more. Everything the Golden Knight did was recorded so he went back in his car and drove to the news studio, leaving the tape in their mail box. The next day all over the news was the video of the Golden Knight, and news reporters said, "This footage was dropped to us this morning. Looks like whoever this is will change the city for the better." Gan drove to a restaurant to eat some breakfast, and everyone inside was reading the newspaper about the Golden Knight. The TV was on in the restaurant, and the news reports were saying that "the police arrested the six men who were drug smugglers. The drugs that were burned were worth about two million dollars on the street.

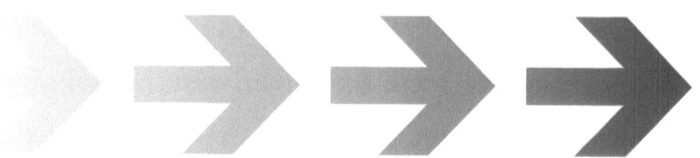

Inside the mental institution Mack Sub was watching the news and was angry with what was going on. He called the attendant to come and give him a shot, so the attendant unlocked the door and Mack Sub charged at him and gave the shot to the attendant. The attendant was knocked out on the floor as Mack Sub took his clothes and changed into them. Mack Sub, now dressed as an attendant, locked his cell door and walked to the elevator. No one in the institution recognized Mack Sub, so he just walked out of the institution. When the attendant inside of Mack Sub's cell woke up he was screaming, which got the attention of other workers, and they unlocked the door for him. That's when the alarms went off in the institution. Everybody was yelling a patient was missing, and they found out it was Mack Sub.

The mental institution called the F.B.I. and told them what happened, and somehow word got out to the press and it was all over TV; Mack Sub escaped. The police looked at all the cameras in the institution and saw how Mack Sub escaped by dressing as an attendant. The F.B.I. had no idea where to start looking, so they put out a wanted ad for Mack Sub all over the TV saying, "Mack Sub is eighty years old, he escaped from a mental institution, if anyone sees him please notify your police station, thank you." Back in Guatemala City Zona Viva, Gan was on the computer reading the breaking news. He realized Mack Sub would be coming here since he lost two million in drug money.

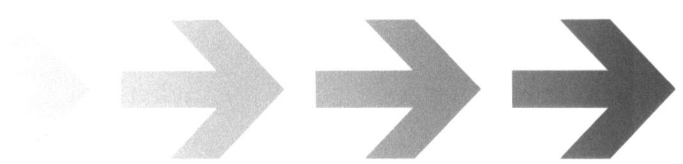

The next day Gan drove to a shopping mall in the city to buy things he needed for the house. Once he stepped in the mall he realized it was under the control of mobsters. They were all shady characters with guns, knives, and small bombs. They lined up every person in the mall and pointed guns at them. One of the mobsters saw Gan and aimed his gun at him and said, "You come in this group now and sit down." The mobsters were taking all the money from the stores in the mall and held the people hostage so the police wouldn't interfere. As Gan was sitting down with the hostages he was counting how many mobsters there were in the mall. The total of mobsters he counted was thirty, and that worried him. There were too many to fight, and even if he would escape someone would notice and shoot him. Without the knight suit he was powerless so he just sat there waiting for an opportunity to arise so he could escape. The mobsters gathered all the money in bags and were waiting for a truck to come and pick them up. The mobsters were nervous, because the truck that was going to pick them up didn't show up yet. Gan looked at all the mobsters and noticed how most of them had their guns on their belts rather than in their hands. This was what Gan was waiting for; he got up and ran as fast as he could to the other exit of the mall. The mobsters took out their guns and followed him, but it was no good; Gan made it to his car and drove out of the mall to his house.

He got the knight suit and drove back to the mall, and he saw the truck the mobsters were talking about pull into the mall's parking lot. He followed them and then he got out of his car, and the two men came out of the truck and the Golden Knight grabbed them and the taser sensors went off and shocked the men and they fell to the floor. The Golden Knight walked into the mall's back entrance, where he escaped and slowly hid behind the walls. He turned on his heat seeker and saw the thirty mobsters at the front entrance. The Golden Knight moved closer and closer until he heard the mobsters talking, saying, "The truck is outside; let's go." All of the mobsters went outside except for two. The two stood behind and planted a big bomb in the entrance of the mall and walked out. The hostages were yelling and panicking as the two mobsters locked the front entrance doors.

 The Golden Knight approached the hostages and said, "Run to the back exit of the mall," but the hostages looked at him and were even more afraid. He said to them again, "I am here to save you, now please run to the back exit, you will be safe." The hostages finally listened and everyone got out of the building alive. The bomb exploded, and the entire mall came crashing down on the Golden Knight. The mobsters were in the truck in the parking lot observing the damaged they caused. The two men who were driving the truck woke up and told the rest of the mobsters that the hostages were outside of the building. They thought to themselves, "How were the hostages able to get out?" and that's when they see this Golden figure walking out of the rubble.

    The mobsters got out of the truck and walked slowly toward this Golden figure. Thirty mobsters came with pointed guns at the figure. The figure said, "I am the Golden Knight, and you will pay for making a building fall on me." The Golden Knight charged at the mobsters and ten fell to the floor immobilized due to the taser sensors. The rest of the mobsters kept shooting but soon realized that it was no good. The Golden Knight punched all of them, and thirty mobsters were immobilized against one Golden Knight. The hostages couldn't believe what they saw. The police came and the hostages told them everything that happened, and the money from the mall was in police custody since there was no building to put it in and all the mobsters were in jail.

 Gan drove back home and decided to leave the Golden Knight suit in the trunk of his car incase a situation like the mall one happened again. So one suit was in the car and the other was in the secret room. Gan turned on the news and was happy to see how the Golden Knight was well-known in the city. One news report states, "People are carrying cameras to record the Golden Knight's heroic deeds." Gan continues watching as a news reporter said, "One of the hostages in the mall explosion recorded the Golden Knight's fight with thirty mobsters and recorded the Knight walking out of the rubble of the exploded building. What you see here is actual footage from the mall explosion, and you see how not even a falling building can stop the Golden Knight from putting the bad guys away."

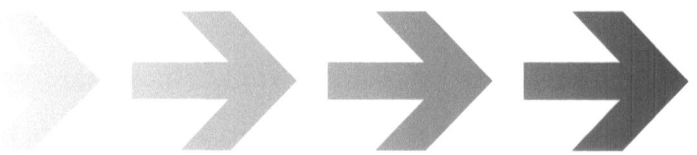

Back in Guatemala City Zona Viva, Mack Sub orders a meeting with all the drug lords and mobsters. They are talking about how much business they are losing ever since the Golden Knight came. Mack Sub says, "I want this Golden Knight dead! Speak to the government; they might know something about this Golden Knight. After all, we pay them to keep quiet. Go see what they know." The mobsters go talk to the governor about the Knight. However, the governor dismisses them, saying, "We have no more business with you." The mobsters return to Mack Sub, telling him what happened. The old man flips out and starts shooting the mobsters. Mack Sub says, "We paid them all these years to look the other way, and now when some guy dressed as a knight puts our boys in jail and shows a little justice they have a change of heart!" The drug lords and remaining mobsters are looking at Mack Sub as he continues, saying, "We will kill the governor and then we will hunt down the Golden Knight."

The Adventures of One Man

Several days passed by, and Gan turned on the news and breaking news was on. Reporters were talking about the murder of the governor. Gan turns up the volume on the TV as the reporter says, "People are panicking as mobsters take over the city, killing anyone in their way." As the reporter starts to talk, a mobster comes up from behind and shoots the reporter. The mobster is on TV and says into the camera, "Golden Knight, wherever you are, you must come out and face us or there won't be a city left to save." Gan ran to his car and put the Golden Knight suit on and drove into the city. In the city he saw fires and bloodshed all around. People were inside their cars, trapped in fires, and bodies of people were everywhere on the floor. One mobster came out of hiding and stood in front of the Golden Knight's car, aiming a rocket at it. He fired the rocket and the car blew up. Smoke and fire was everywhere, and the mobsters were laughing. The Golden Knight came out of the fire and smoke and ran toward the mobster and grabbed him, yelling, "Who did this to the city?" Jolts of electricity flow into the mobster, and he now loses consciousness.

That's when Mack Sub walks into the area, and he approaches the Golden Knight saying, "You amaze me. I can't kill you. Nothing can hurt you, it seems." Mack Sub walks closer to the Golden Knight and pulls out a small glass jar. He opens it and throws it on the suit, and immediately the suit starts melting away. The Golden Knight takes off the remaining suit, revealing his identity. Mack Sub smiles and smacks him to the ground, dragging him inside the hotel. Gan awakens, tied to a chair, as Mack Sub walks in and says, "You are a true survivor, Gan. I had no idea you were the Golden Knight until I melted away your suit. I can't believe you would try to stop me, and I will give you credit; you almost did. You gave this city hope. Even the corrupt governor changed his ways, and you had an impact on people's lives. I bet you're wondering how I was able to melt away your suit. After all, it can't be destroyed. You're probably wondering how I know so much. Well, I'll tell you. Back in China I had a Chinese girl named Winnie Chow who worked for the same technology unit you did. She was my inside eyes to secrets of Chinese military technology. She stumbled on the weakness on the knight suit and kept it a secret from the Chinese government. Do you want to know the secret? The secret is in the Golden Poison frog. Its skin is drenched in alkaloid poison. This poison prevents nerves from transmitting impulses, leaving the muscles in an inactive state of contraction. To put it simply, the poison can lead to heart failure and nervous shaking of muscle fibers. One milligram of poison can kill ten to twenty humans. The only reason you're still alive is because the poison was on the suit instead of your skin."

Gan asks, "How did you find this?" That's when Mack Sub's scientist Winnie Chow comes inside and says, "Indigenous cultures like the Chocó Embera people in Colombia's rainforest use the frog's poison in darts for hunting. They carefully expose the frog to the heat of a fire, and the frog exudes small amounts of poisonous fluid."

Mack Sub interrupts, saying, "We found the weakness for the suit. Now the Chinese will pay much money to keep this a secret and I will be getting richer and more powerful." Mack Sub walks to Gan and says "goodbye" as he tells his scientist, who is also an assassin, to kill Gan. Mack Sub leaves the hotel meeting room, and the assassin walks up to Gan. She takes her knife and cuts the rope off of him and she says to him, "My name is Winnie Chow. I work for the F.B.I. in the United States. They sent me here to warn you about Mack Sub's escape. I didn't get here in time to tell you Mack Sub wants you dead for costing him two million in drug money." She opens the door and takes Gan to her hotel room so they can talk. Gan asked her, "How can we stop him? The entire city is in ruin, and everyone here is dead."

Winnie Chow and Gan drive to his house. He puts on the suit and tells her to stay here for her safety, so she did. Gan drove back to the city and Mack Sub's men were shooting at him. The Golden Knight ran toward them and shocked all them until they were unconscious. Mack Sub came out into the street to see what was happening, and he was shaking as the Golden Knight approached him.

Mack Sub asked him, "So you are going to kill me and get your revenge for what I did to you?"The Golden Knight answers, "I am not going to kill you and I am not going to seek revenge." Mack Sub is confused and asks, "Why won't you just kill me already? I mean, even your father didn't want to. You would think after all I put your family through you would kill me, but both of you hesitate. Why?" The Golden Knight takes off his helmet, revealing his face, and said, "I am a man just like you. Even though I have the power to kill you, I will not. The power to take another man's life is not mine but God's, and he is the only one that has that right." As they were talking, it began to rain harder and faster than ever, and lighting shot throughout the sky and thunder roared, making standing outside very dangerous. Gan puts his helmet back on and slowly walks away from Mack Sub.

Mack Sub yells, "Where are you going we; are not done yet?" The Golden Knight turns toward him and says, "Get out of the storm, it will kill you," but Mack Sub takes out his glass jar filled with poison from the frog and slowly walks toward the Golden Knight. The Golden Knight says, "After all I said to you and even spare your life you still want to kill me?" Mack Sub is about to open the glass jar when lightning strikes him. The eighty-year-old man fell to the floor and the poison fell on him. Gan walked toward him and realized that Mack Sub had died. The F.B.I. came and arrested all the drug lords and mobsters.

Gan and Winnie Chow got married and moved to Florida to live by his grandparents' house. Even with all the chaos and fighting gone in Gan's life he still puts on the Golden Knight suit and saves people from crime, giving them hope for a better tomorrow.

The End

www.ingramcontent.com/pod-product-compliance
Ingram Content Group UK Ltd.
Pitfield, Milton Keynes, MK11 3LW, UK
UKHW042004230426
12048UKWH00009B/530